CASTLE MOUNTAIN

KATHRYN HARTLEY

Published by Cougar Books, January 2024

ISBN: 9781777872526

Typeset: Greg Salisbury

Book Cover Design: Gayll Morrison - www.gayllery.biz

Portrait Photographer: Gayll Morrison - www.gayllery.biz

Dedicated to my son, Jordan,
who always loved this story.

CONTENTS

CHAPTER 1

MORNING COMES EARLY

Dad is at my bedroom door calling: "Wakey, wakey. Rise and shine, kid. The world isn't gonna wait for you to sleep the day away."

I hear him down the hall knocking on Chloe's door and Matt's, then he clumps down the stairs singing his silly old holiday song.

The 24th of May,
The Queen's Birthday,
If we don't get a holiday
We'll all run away.

He gets caught by a coughing fit at the end and I jam my pillow over my ears to cover the guttural sounds he makes when he coughs. When it's quiet I struggle out of bed, feeling bruised and sick from not enough sleep. I don't mind hiking so much but I really hate getting up in the middle of the night. Hiking season always starts, in our family, on the May 24th long weekend. And always when the sun is barely over the horizon.

If I don't get up now, though, Chloe will be hogging the bathroom and the whole day will be ruined. I'll be the last one to breakfast and the last one ready to go and she'll bug me about it all day. I get dressed quickly in a clean pair of shorts and my butterfly T-shirt, also fresh from the wash. Everything has to be clean, clean, clean around here; even to go climbing around on mountains. I grab a light wind-breaker from my closet and open the bedroom door. At that same moment, as if she's been waiting for me, Chloe opens hers across the hall and races for the bathroom. I start to a run as soon as I see her but I'm not quite fast enough. I get to the door just as it closes in my face. I grab the handle and wiggle it and yell, "Chloe!!"

"What is all that racket?" Mom is at the foot of the stairs yelling up at us. "You kids just get dressed and get down here. I want to be on the road by 9:00. Did you hear me?"

Nobody answers her. Through the door I hear Chloe running water and singing "As It Was". She says she is in love with Harry Styles. I think he looks like a bum, always showing off his tattoos all over himself. And when he sings he sounds like he's whining. She hates me when I say that.

"You don't know anything. You're only nine and pretty stupid at that. Just wait till you grow up," she said to me yesterday when she was putting up a new Harry poster in her room. "Then you'll find out what it's all about."

"Oh yeah?!" I stood in the doorway with just a toe sticking into her room. If she saw the toe I knew she would scream at me. Her room was off limits to Matt and me but she always came into my room whenever she wanted to. I couldn't stop her. "Yeah?" I said. "And you're so smart? Fourteen isn't grown up either you know. And he's still weird." I ran down the hall and just missed being hit by a shoe she threw through the door.

So, since I can't get into the bathroom, I go downstairs to have some breakfast even though I don't really want any; it's too early. Mom has made oatmeal. I knew she would. I hate oatmeal! It's so pale and gluey and dead looking.

"Well," Dad says. "And how's my Pumpkin this morning?"

"Okay, I guess."

"Okay!? You should be more than okay on a glorious morning like this. Look at that. The sun is shining, the sky is blue, the birds are singing and all us chickens are up and ready for a great hike."

"Daddy," I groan. "The sun isn't even UP yet!"

"Well, you know what they say? 'The early bird gets the worm'. You should be happy to be up before the sun." He ruffled my hair then sat down at the end of the table.

"I'm not a bird," I said. "And worms are gross."

"You're not? Huh. Could have fooled me." he says and goes back to his coffee.

I peer into the oatmeal pot. "Yuch!"

"You'd better have some, Joanie. You'll be hungry if you don't," Mom says.

"Don't want any."

I am just sitting down with a glass of juice and a piece of raisin toast when Chloe comes thumping down the stairs. The sweet hot cinnamon smell of toasted raisin bread obviously got to her.

"You little creep," she says when she spies the piece of toast half-way to my mouth. "I bet you took the last piece of raisin bread, didn't you?"

I don't answer but just bite down really hard into the toast and give her a dirty look.

"I don't know why you had to go and have her!" she says to Mom. "She's such a pain!"

"And good morning to you too," Mom says. "Is your brother up yet?"

"I think I heard him snorting around in his room."

"Joanie," Dad says, "Go get your brother up. Tell him I want him down here now or we're leaving without him."

"Ah, Dad," I say, but I go, thumping my feet down hard on every stair just to let him know I hate doing this.

CHAPTER 2

INTO THE BEAR'S DEN

Matt is still curled under his covers like a hibernating bear. I pull the blankets down and pinch his ear. His room smells of sweat and old socks.

"Matthew! Get up, lazy," I say. "It's the middle of the night already and we all have to get up. Dad says if you don't get up now we're going without you."

"So go without me," he growls at me and jerks the covers back over his ear.

I turn around and bounce down hard on the side of his bed. When he doesn't move I bounce a couple more times and punch his shoulder.

"Dad says!" I yell into his ear.

"Get lost, shit-head," he growls.

"Dad!" I yell. "Matt swore at me! He said shit-head!"

"You little snitch. I'll get you..."

I am out the door as fast as the covers fly off the bed. Then I hear Dad coming up the stairs so I wait in the hall. I don't want to miss this.

"You are getting up and dressed this minute, young man! And I don't want to hear about any more swearing in this house," Dad says.

"I'm not going," Matt says sulkily. "I'm sick"

"You're not sick. It's your own fault. If you didn't stay up so late watching videos you'd feel fine. You knew darn well we were going to Banff this morning. Think ahead a little bit. When are you going to grow up and start acting like a adult? You're 15 years old and you still act like a kid!"

" I act like a kid 'cause you treat me like a kid," Matt grumbles. I am crouched outside the door and expect Dad to start yelling at this. He doesn't though. It sounds like he is trying hard not to.

"And what do you mean by that?" Dad growls.

"Well, you still won't let me drive the car."

"As far as I'm concerned it's up to you to prove to me that you can be responsible. Now come on, get up and let's make this a good family day. No grumbling."

Then Matt pushes it just an inch too far when he says,

"You told Joanie if I didn't get up you'd go without me…"

I hear the quick rustle of movement and Dad yells, "That's it! You get moving! And I mean now! Downstairs in five minutes!"

He starts to cough like he always does now when he yells and he comes out into the hallway and just about trips over me. He is coughing so hard his eyes are watering and he is spitting into a Kleenex. I sneak a look into Matt's room where he's standing in his underwear, throwing clothes out of his closet onto his bed. I hear him muttering, "Shit, shit, shit," but I don't tell on him this time. I follow Dad downstairs and into the kitchen. I sit down at the table again but Mom grabs my arm all of a sudden and it hurts.

"Now look what you've done," she hisses. I look at her.

"What did I do?" I ask. I don't mean to be snotty to her but I really don't know.

"You know perfectly well; getting your Father upset like that," she whispers, nodding over to where Dad is pouring himself another cup of coffee at the stove, holding his Kleenex to his lips. "You know he's not well! Why do you think I asked you kids to take it easy on him?"

"I didn't. It wasn't my fault. It was Matt!" I feel my eyes getting hot but I don't want to cry in front of Chloe so I try to get mad instead. I look down at my plate and grind my teeth together so hard my jaw hurts. Mom is quiet for a minute and I hear Dad take his coffee into the bathroom and close the door. We can still hear him coughing. We've heard our parents discuss our Dad's smoking many times. He knows he should quit. He just doesn't.

Mom lets go of my arm and says softly, "You kids are just going to have to learn to manage without running to your Father for every little thing. All right?"

I nod and Chloe kicks me under the table like this is all my fault. Matt comes thumping down the stairs and glares at me. He grabs a piece of bread and peanut butter which he eats standing up at the kitchen window. He has his earbuds on and is listening to his favorite streaming channel so loud I can hear it over here. I don't care if he does go deaf.

Finally I get a chance to get into the bathroom but I'm still the last one ready, as usual.

It's 9:30 before we're all ready and the lunch is packed into the backpack that Dad will carry. Dad always starts out with the pack because it's always been his job but I know it won't be long before he gets tired and hands it over to Matt.

CHAPTER 3

WE'RE GOING WHERE?

Mom gets out the hiking book and we sit at the kitchen table so she can show us where we're going. The book always goes with us. It has raggedy edges from being looked at so much and, on almost every second page, Mom has put little notes in the margin about what the hikes were like and who went on them and when we went. I don't know what difference it makes because she never wants to do the same one twice so why do we have to know all this stuff?

She shows us the route for today up the shoulder of Castle Mountain. It sounds like an exciting, romantic place with a name like that.

"Are you serious?" Chloe says. "That looks impossible."

"Yeah. Why don't we just climb right up to the top of the castle and plant a flag?" Matt's voice drips with sarcasm.

"All right you two. Why don't we at least give it a shot," says Dad. I can feel his warm breath stirring my hair as he stands behind me. His breath smells of coffee and cough drops. He sounds kind of tired and I wonder if he really wants to go at all. He's never very excited about our family hikes anymore because he's always so tired but he still goes. I can kind of understand it because I think he feels he'll be letting the whole family down if he doesn't go.

Once we're on the road I cheer up. Matt and Chloe are arguing about whose turn it is to get a window seat. Dad, as usual, has a cigarette smoking away as he drives. I want to be by a window so I can see out and have the fresh air blow in my face to get rid of the smoke but Mom says, "Joanie, you sit in the middle this time. You can have a window on the way back."

"Ah, Mom. I sat in the middle last time."

"Last time was last September. I bet you don't even remember last time," Chloe says, poking me in the ribs.

"Do too. It's not fair," I grumble, but I crawl over Chloe's lap to give her the window. I let my elbow kind of hit her in the head as I climb over and she hits me back but I just make a face and ignore her.

"I don't want the window on the way back," I complain. "What if we don't come back at all? What if we get eaten by bears or something?"

"Well then you certainly won't have to worry about it, will you? Now settle down and look out the window." With that Mom turns around abruptly and that's that.

"I can't look out a window. I don't have a window. Chloe and Matt have the windows, like always," I grumble under my breath. Matt sticks out his tongue at me and I make a face back.

I twist in my seatbelt until I can kneel on the seat facing backwards and look through the back window. I know it scares Dad when I do this and he'll yell if he catches me. He thinks I'll get killed or something if he has to stop the car suddenly. I don't care; it's the only window I get so I lean against the back of the seat and rest my chin on my arms. The road keeps appearing in a long strip from under the car like a carpet unrolling very fast and disappearing again into the distance behind us.

The sun is spreading its pink light along the edge of the sky. There aren't very many other cars on the highway this early in the morning. I pretend we're the only ones left after a planetary disaster. The world is totally empty of people. Except for us. Some terrible disaster has wiped out everybody else and we can go anywhere and do anything we want. We can go into stores and take anything we like and sleep in any nice house we see. Maybe I'd have the terrible disaster happen to Chloe, too.

Matt is still sulking scrunched up in the corner of the car with his earbuds on hardly even looking out the window. Chloe is watching YouTube on her phone. What the heck did they want a window seat for if that's all they're going to do? I'm just opening my mouth to say something nasty about not using the window when I catch Mom's glance in the rear view mirror and I know she has had enough for now. I shut up.

"Turn around and sit properly, Joanie."

I scowl but squiggle around and slouch down in my seat.

CHAPTER 4

THE CASTLE

We stop for gas in Canmore then drive around the traffic circle that takes you to Banff. On the highway, just past the Buffalo Paddocks, is a sign that says Warden's Office. I imagine somebody named Warden sitting in his office and looking out his window at the buffalo grazing in the new spring grass.

Gravel crunches and spits as we pull into the parking area where the hike starts. It's a big lot and empty. I wonder how many other people really do this sort of thing. I think it's kind of weird to climb a mountain just so you can climb back down but that's what we're going to do apparently. I look up at the mountain through the trees. I can't believe anything can really be that tall. The spires pierce the sky and are surrounded by little floating clouds.

Dad heaves the pack onto his back and gives me the canteen to carry. It doesn't feel heavy at first but the more we walk along the tree-lined path, the heavier it gets. And we aren't even at the mountain yet. We march together up the trail.

The forest smells are tangy in the morning air. I try to pick out the scents of pine, cedar, wet dirt, rotting logs, and just plain fresh air.

After a while I start to notice how the sunlight does crisp and peculiar things on the leaves and rocks this early in the morning. I peer into the forest and watch it shimmer in and out of focus between the trees. I want to look in all directions at once but the others are far ahead already so I have to run. Dad's old army knapsack whisks in and out of the trees just up the trail. Pretty soon my stomach starts to grumble. I'm hungry already and I know Chloe and Matt are drooling and following the knapsack with their eyes but I know none of us will say anything about being hungry or tired. Mom and Dad expect us to keep marching no matter what.

Castle Mountain towers above us a massive wall of stone. There are huge columns spaced along the expanse that really do look like the turrets of a giant's castle. I can't believe we are going to walk across the shoulder of this mountain. Not in one day. There must be a hotel or something where we can rest and have something hot to eat and watch Netflix. Hiking is fun, Mom says. But looking up at what I can see of Castle Mountain it looks like something from the moon and not much fun at all.

Then I see the giant who lives in the castle! He is massive. He must have been sitting down behind his walls because as he stands up his head, then his shoulders, then his hips rise above the highest peak of the mountain. His shaggy head blocks out the sun. How does no one else see him? His huge fingers curl over the edge of the mountain as he prepares to climb over the ridge. I hold my hand up to stop him. He pauses and looks down at me. His eye alone is larger than my whole head but I have powers that nobody knows about. I send a calming blue light zipping up to the giant and immediately I see him yawn a huge yawn. The sound of his yawn is like the roar of a massive engine. I hope my family will think it's just a truck down on the highway. The giant slowly, sleepily sinks back behind his walls.

Gasping I catch up with my brother. "Do you really think we are going to do it, Matt?"

"Sure," Matt says in a gruff imitation of Dad. "We

can do anything we set our minds to. Whatsa' matter? You tired already? We've only been out a little while. We've got a long way to go yet."

I growl at him and slump back to the rear. He thinks he's so tough but I know he'll be the very first to start whining for lunch. I am going to show him, and Chloe too. I'm strong. I know I can handle this. We go hiking every summer but Matt complains every time. He's always grumbling about being hungry. Actually he's not so bad as brothers go. Most of my friends have brothers, some older, some younger. All of them are a pain but at least Matt will help sometimes if I get into trouble.

Chloe's the real pain. On hikes Chloe's always the one who gets blisters and has to sit down and rub her feet every two seconds. She wears Funky Punkers, usually new, instead of well washed trainers like me. She has to look stylish even out here where there's nobody to see her but the bears.

When we left the car in the early, grey light Chloe was beside me for a while as we marched up the trail behind the bobbing backpack.

"Do you think we can do it?" I asked, trying to be friendly. She could be so mean it was smart to start the day as friends.

"Yup. At least I can," she said. "And you better not whine all the way like a baby either. You bug me."

"Well, you bug me too and I don't whine!" I retorted, all friendly resolve splintering in the sunlight.

"You do too. You make everybody mad when you whine."

"I don't whine," I complained. "You're just saying that to make me mad. Just for that I won't let you have any of my chocolate bar at lunch."

"I don't care about your stupid chocolate bar," she said. But I knew she did. She claimed to be on a diet and always asked Mom not to pack anything sweet but Mom would bring something for me and Matt then when Chloe couldn't stand it, she would steal mine. I usually let her because, at fourteen, she's bigger and stronger than me.

CHAPTER 5

A CABIN IN THE WOODS

I wander along the trail alone now. I'm not scared. I know that bears are more scared of me than I am of them. Besides, bears don't look all that big in the zoo and I run pretty fast. I'm on the track team at school.

The poplar trees send tiny white feathers floating on the wind. I can't feel any breeze against my bare arm but somehow they fly in the still air. I realize what's happening. Those are fairy helicopters. The tiny fairies are sailing through the air operating the miniature helicopters. I reach out to try to catch one but the fairy piloting that one makes a quick right turn and is out of reach before I can close my fingers.

The trail is following beside a stream now. The water

sucks with hollow burps and slurping sounds under an overhanging rock. The water reflects back all the colors of the forest and sky. It looks as though someone spilled a box of oil paints on the water. I tried that once. The paint stayed in all the separate colors, never mixing, floating on the surface of the water. I'd like to just sit here on the rock and watch the sunlight dancing up from the water in bright, moving freckles that sparkle on the grey rocks. It would be so quiet.

I would be safe here from Chloe's teasing, from Mom's eyes that see through me all the time, from Matt and his bullying, from having to pretend all the time at school that I'm popular and cool and at home that I am perfect. It would be so great if Dad and I could build a little cabin in a place like this and live in it always and I would read and go for long walks with him.

We'd build our cabin out of the pine trees that fill this forest. I took a wood carving class at summer camp one time. We cut and peeled branches from trees down by the lake. We used special tools to peel the bark. I remember that woodsy smell and the feel of the silky soft layer underneath the bark that was still wet with sap. We could make our cabin out of logs peeled like that. Inside we would have a wood stove that would crackle and glow all the time. We'd grow vegetables in a garden out front in the sunshine. Hikers would come by on the trail and stop to visit. They would always have food to share. Oh, and a dog. We would need a dog for protection. A big fluffy dog.

In our private world his cough would be gone because of all the fresh air. He would hold my hand and show me the stars in the black velvet sky at night just like he used to when I was little.

He was different then. When he looks at me now his eyes don't really seem to be focused. It's as if he only half sees you, like you're a ghost. I miss him. I know that sounds funny when he's right up the trail there, following behind Mom in the spring sunlight. I think there is something wrong with him. When he breathes it sounds like the vacuum cleaner does when you sucked up something you're not supposed to and it gets stuck. I'm scared to ask him, though.

I asked Mom one day and she said, "Hush, Joanie. There's nothing wrong with your father. He smokes too much, that's all." Except I didn't believe her because she is being really careful around him now and she keeps telling us not to upset him.

On these hikes it's always Mom who picks them, Mom who organizes them, Mom who strides like a trooper while Dad drops further and further behind, contesting my spot as the caboose. He usually wins by whispering in my ear that he has to walk at the end to protect us from wild animals that might creep up behind us and eat us one by one. I always thought that was funny but I let Dad play his game and I pretend to scream and run when he comes up behind me and growls.

So far today he is still way up ahead of me, a blue spot beside the yellow spot that is Mom, with two smaller spots walking behind. I can see Chloe's dangling earrings flashing in the sunlight.

CHAPTER 6

CLIMBING THE MOUNTAIN

We're climbing now. The path veers upwards and it makes walking harder. Mom is marching at the head of the line. She's so strong she scares me sometimes. I don't mean that she IS scary but it's like she wants Chloe and me to be like her. To be strong and confident. I don't know if I know how. I try not complain very much and I refuse to cry when I get hurt; no matter what Chloe says.

Chloe seems to think that being strong means being tough and mean. It's not just me she's mean to either. I've seen her with her friends at school. She's always giving them orders and she teases them about the way they look or the clothes they wear. They all try to be like her; just like she tries to be like Mom.

I don't want to be like Chloe. If I had to be like somebody else I would pick Dad. He is so gentle and nice. He likes to be quiet with me sometimes. Sometimes we go to the store together and he will walk along holding my hand and just squeeze it every once in a while to let me know he knows I am there but we don't talk unless I see a dog or a bird or something and then I'll whisper to Dad and point. He smiles and takes another puff of his cigarette.

Blue smoke always circles his head. If he is in the same room with you for a long time it gets so you can't see very clearly and your eyes start to water. And it makes him cough. He usually sends me out for cough drops when I come home from school. I don't take my coat off when I come home now because I know he will ask me to run over to the store. I don't mind though; he always gives me a quarter every time.

Today his little blue cloud is puffing along behind Mom and it looks kind of nice and homey in among the green trees.

Beside the river, fans of green pine boughs have sparkling underbellies where they hang above the water. I can hear a crazy buzzing overhead and I walk slowly with my head back watching the progress of a little plane that is struggling across the sky. It seems to be on a collision course with two hawks that look like they are exactly the same size as the plane but, suddenly, they pass across each other as though they weren't even in the same world. No feathers erupt.

"Joan...Joanieee..." My name floats down from far ahead. I look around and feel a delicious thrill of fear in my bladder that makes me want to pee when I realize I am entirely alone and I can't even see them anymore. If a bear did come they wouldn't be able to get back in time to save me.

"I'm not afraid of bears," I say out loud. Then louder I call, "I'm coming!", and break into a trot. I scramble over rocks and tree roots that jut like turtles across the trail. The trail is climbing up and away from the river and the valley and the comfort of the car.

Once I made the mistake of saying I wanted to stay in the car and not go on the hike. They said "Okay" and just left me there. By the time they had disappeared between the trees I was out of the car and racing up the trail. I practically ran the whole trail that time and had to wait for them at the top where the ice-cold lake met the glacier at the end of that trail.

There is Dad's bright blue T-shirt. I catch up and

pass him. I can hear his heavy breathing over the tramp of our feet.

"Hey little sparrow," he says, "Did you catch lots of worms this morning?"

"Daddy!"

"Okay. You're a little bird that doesn't like worms. But you know what? I bet if you wanted to you could spread your little wings and fly to the top of that mountain."

I look up at the Castle and imagine soaring up above the trees, above the highest peaks and into the blue, blue sky. I feel the wind in my wing feathers. Far below is the hiking family. They look so tiny from up here.

"Adventure is the best part of life, Kiddo. Did I ever tell you about the time I hiked the Camino trail in Spain with my college buddy? Now that was an adventure. It took us over a month to hike it. It's over 800 kilometers."

"Where did you sleep?"

"We had camping gear and a tent with us. We just stepped off the trail and set up camp when we were tired."

"Did you eat roots and berries in the woods like a bear?" I notice he was having to pause and take a deep breath after just about every sentence.

"We carried as much food as we could in our packs. Then we'd visit the little villages along the way. People were great. If there was no restaurant folks would just invite us to share a meal or even a bed for the night."

It's hard to hear him above the soprano whoosh of my own breathing and the sound of five pairs of feet on the trail. I am not sure if he even cares whether I hear him or not. Sometimes I'm not sure if he's talking to me, or to himself..

After a while Dad starts coughing again and stops to rest on a big rock. I want to sit with him but he motions us kids to go on ahead. Chloe and Matt and I try to stay three abreast on the tiny path, pushing each other roughly into the trees. We fight quietly so Mom won't stop us. She's waiting for us around the next bend. "Where is your father?"

"He's guarding us from the bears," I tell her.

"Old Pop gave up already," Chloe sneers. "He's way back on the trail."

"We'd better wait then," sighs Mom worriedly.

We're quiet for a while, listening to the conversations of the birds in the tree tops. Swallows dive above us, catching their breakfast. Thousands of midges are hovering in the air, catching the sunlight in their wings. The swallows zip through the midges making them swirl like puffs of smoke.

Pretty soon we see the army pack bobbing along

up the trail and Dad catches up. He stops to rest with us for a few minutes and puts the pack on the ground. Matt and Chloe and I look at each other out of the corners of our eyes, knowing what treasures lie inside that pack, wondering who is going to be the first to complain of being hungry. We are always trying to be tougher or stronger or smarter or faster than each other. Matt almost always wins because he's older but sometimes we don't count him, because he's a boy, and it's just Chloe and I. We are pretty even although I'm younger.

As we set off again we both take longer and longer steps until we pass Mom and Dad and we are huffing up the trail in the lead.

Soon the game becomes boring and I deliberately let Chloe get ahead. She tosses her head at me as she races up the trail and out of sight. I hope she gets eaten by a bear.

CHAPTER 7

DAY DREAMS, LUNCH AND
A BIG RED DOG

The trail levels out a little here and I catch my breath and sniff the woods like a young deer. The sweet baked smells of hot grass and pine and mountain daisies begin to rise in the late morning air. The grumble and creak of the tall spruce rubbing together in the wind sounds like a grizzly bear ambling sloppily through the brush; breaking and bending anything between him and breakfast. I'm not worried. He'll get Chloe first.

The path winds around the shoulder of an old avalanche area. Moss has crept up over the rocks and miniature pine trees are sprouting among the cracks. Some of the old logs sleep forever under their emerald coats of moss. They look so soft I want to lie down and stare up at the pale sky until the moss creeps over me too. I would sleep for a hundred years and then... then I would jump up, transformed into an incredibly gorgeous girl, like a stubby little caterpillar becomes a beautiful butterfly.

I would go down into the world and conquer everyone with my mystery and my beauty. "Where did she come from?" they would cry to each other. And I would be dressed all in purple bells of wild iris with a long woven scarf of fire weed and earrings of buttercups dangling and flashing beneath long, blond hair. I would break boys' hearts and all the boys that Chloe has a crush on would be madly in love with me instead. I would not bother with them, though.

I would be a passionate artist who lived and worked in an enormous studio high above the city. Chloe could work for me. She would sell my work. I would never bother with such things.

I shiver. Actually it is getting colder as we climb even though it's almost noon now. I can hear Matt just ahead complaining to Mom: "Don't you think we should stop soon and have lunch? Joanie isn't going to make it much further; you know how tired she gets."

"I do not!" I try to shout, but just then, because

I'm not looking where I'm going, my foot catches in the intricate lace-work of tangled roots and I hit the ground with a sickening thump!

Dad, close on my heels, picks me up and swings me onto my feet. I'm disappointed. If I was smaller he would have swung me up onto his shoulders and we would have walked along like that with me towering over everything and bumping along feeling his bony shoulders under me like a horse. I would ride so high in the air on Dad's back that I could look down on Chloe's head and see the uneven dark part in her hair. The bees would think I was a strange bird and dive bomb me. It makes me sad to think that he can't do that anymore. I wonder if he ever did that with Chloe. I guess he must have. I wonder if she remembers.

I hate her for being born before me. I wish she hadn't been born at all, then I would be the only girl in the family. I would be more special then.

I dream of riding a tall white stallion along the trail; my long, silver hair blowing like a cloak behind me. My magnificent army follows and we are pouring over this mountain pass to reclaim my kingdom. My army will deal out justice and send the enemy running to hide. The enemy would be anyone I didn't like; the teachers at school (most of them anyway), boys who tease me, girls who make smart cracks in the showers at school. Chloe would be the worst. We would capture her and make her my slave.

Finally we stop for lunch. As soon as we stop Dad digs in his pocket for a pack of Du Maurier cigarettes. The pack flashes red in the sun and Mom frowns at him but he lights one and the wheezing in his chest eases with the first few puffs. He knows it's the cigarettes that make him so out of breath all the time but he can't stop. The smoke floats, blue and pungent, into the mountain air. I sneak up close to him and breath in the smoke, trying to understand the magic of cigarettes. I don't know why he likes to breath smoke. It's like acid in my throat. I have friends at school who smoke. I doubt if they like it either but they do it anyway. They think it's cool. I don't. I think it's stupid.

We sit on cold grey rocks at a lookout where the trail turns and seems to disappear up the slopes. The view across the wide valley we have climbed is so vast it makes my legs shake to see Matt standing right on the ledge that drops into the valley. I want him to come away from there but I don't dare say anything because he would call me a chicken. I stand well back from the ledge and look across the expanse. All the other mountains up and down the valley look as soft and innocent as ice cream sundaes. Castle Mountain, the one we're on, looks hard and cold and huge; not much like a castle at all from here except I remember looking at it from the highway below and thinking I could almost see the flags of a giant king flying from the peaks.

A butter-colored moth flits past me, gently brushing its wings across my cheek. A horsefly dives and whirrs overhead and I flinch at the buzz saw noise, so sudden in the stillness of the mountain forest.

"Lunch, you guys," howls Chloe, digging in the sandwich bag for peanut butter and honey. I'm cold now that we've stopped moving and dig out my sweater from the pack first then wander off to the edge of the clearing with a salmon sandwich in one hand and a dill pickle in the other.

Some people come down the trail and stop to talk to Mom and Dad. They ignore Chloe and Matt but they smile at me because I smile first. They talk to each other in French, then to Mom and Dad in English. They are pointing and saying that the hike becomes difficult after the next stream because there was a recent avalanche that erased parts of the trail.

The man wears a knitted cap pulled down over heavy black hair and trailing sideburns. The woman walks in a long skirt of Indian print cotton with hiking boots peering from beneath the hem. She sports a Brown-eyed Susan drooping in her nest of brown hair. They also have backpacks, slogan T-shirts that say "Save Our Forests", and a red-haired dog.

The dog fascinates me. He looks like he's wearing a woman's wig because his hair is so long and silky looking. His coat is the deep red of cranberries. I don't dare go to him in case he isn't friendly but he trots over to me and sniffs my sandwich. I jerk it back which startles us both and he bounds off to investigate a pile of rabbit pellets.

The sun is higher now and across the valley the miles stretch and shrink like plastic wrap. I can look down on the shining silver thread of the Bow River and, to the south, Mom points out Mount Victoria and the little blue jewel of Lake Louise. Castle Mountain leans above us, watching us sitting on its cold shoulder in the sun. Two dusty, brown butterflies fly together above the grass.

"Are they flying like that because they're mating, do you think?" I whisper to Chloe. Immediately I feel dumb and Chloe laughs. I know better than to think out loud with her around. She doesn't let up.

" You really are a dope, aren't you! "Don't you know

anything? Of course they're mating. Did you think they were having tea?"

"I just asked!" I yell back. "Can't I just ask?!"

Mom tells us both to be quiet. Chloe keeps making smart cracks under her breath. She makes me so mad I am ready to start a fight with her. Chloe never knows when to shut up. I'd like to make her shut up but I know there isn't any point in keeping this up with Mom around. She'll slap one or both us for sure. I put my fingers in my ears and walk away and hum 'Born to be Wild' really loud.

CHAPTER 8

THINGS GET A WHOLE LOT HARDER

After lunch Dad lies back on the grass and closes his eyes. Mom and Chloe are arguing about whether she should have to do dishes on nights when she has homework. Matt is throwing rocks over the edge of the cliff.

I leave them and follow a cricket through the grass. I have to move slowly to let him stay ahead of me. I watch a tiny, red squirrel watching me. A fat bee rides on the swaying pink face of a wild rose.

I wish normal life could always be quiet like this. I don't see why I always have to be DOING something:

doing homework, doing chores. Chloe is always running around doing something, always busy or always out with her friends. That's great for her but if she's not around Mom will pick on me to do things. Whenever she catches me lying on my bed staring at the ceiling or sitting outside watching the sun on the grass, she'll always find something for me to do. Sometimes I wish I was Chloe; other times I wish my sister would just get lost some night and never find her way back to the house.

It seems like Mom is always telling me to get outside and get some exercise and fresh air and stop mooning around the house with my nose in a book. Then when I go outside she complains because I am not around to do errands when she needs me.

Chloe, one time when she was in a good mood, once told me she thought they just liked to have something to yell at us for because they thought that was what being a parent was all about. I know I'm not going to be like that with my kids, if I ever have any. They'll be able to do what they want because I'll remember what it's like to be a kid.

"Joanie, we're off," Mom calls.

The trail is much tougher now. We work our way between trees, hands gripping rough bark and coming away brown and sticky with sap. I rub my fingers together and feel the stickiness roll into miniature logs of gum and bits of bark. I use handles of gooseberry bushes to pull myself up the steep trail, after giving the bush a good tug to make sure the roots are solid. The ground is slippery and chunks of sharp rock are all over everywhere.

The path is so faint we lose it many times. I look up across the expanse of silver rock and see a dead stump thrusting sharp and black into the clear sky. Behind me is a screen of trees. We are cut off from all I know. The desert of broken rock goes on forever. We're going across the avalanche area, the scree, aiming for a tiny shine of blue way at the far end. That must be the lake where we finally can turn around and go home. I hope so. I can't admit it but I'm getting really tired. I focus on that shine of blue.

I am a forest sprite. I live there in the woods beside the turquoise lake. My best friend is a wolf who sleeps curled around me to keep me warm and safe. We are following these people as they hike across our mountain. We know all the dangers of this country and we don't want anything to happen to these people, except maybe the fat one, but we never reveal ourselves to the people either so we follow carefully with the softest of steps.

They will need us before their long journey is through.

It is steep but there are footholds in the rock. My trainers give thin protection from the sharp edges and my feet have to match the sharp angles at each step. I really am beginning to get tired now and wonder how much further we have to go. We still have to go all the way back, too.

I use finger holds in the rocks and hand holds of juniper to pull myself up. There is a scratch on my arm and a little blood dribbles into the sunlight.

I imagine myself covered in a thick, brown coat of heavy fur. I imagine I am sleeping in a warm, dry cave with my stomach full and the cold wind that now whips my hair painfully across my forehead is howling harmlessly outside the cave.

"C'mon, Joanie Moanie. The trail's over here."

"No, it's easier up this way."

"Shouldn't we go back now? Wasn't that the end of the trail where we had lunch?"

"Settle down you three. It isn't far now."

The usual trail nonsense goes on around me. I don't like these people. I will go back up to our wolf cave and leave them to fall off a cliff somewhere. Nobody would ever know. They would think I fell off too and they would all leave me alone.

We're starting to find patches of snow now, even though it's May. We're so high up on the mountain that the snow never gets warm enough to melt. We have actually moved around behind the shoulder of the mountain now and we haven't been able to see the valley or the highway for a long time. The birds are quiet too, or there are no birds. The river still sings somewhere behind us even though we can't hear it through the blanket of trees.

Dad asked me once if a tree fell in a forest and there was no one there to hear it, did it really make any sound? It seemed like a really silly question to me. Of course it makes a noise; a very loud noise. But today I wonder. Maybe, since I'm right here at this very minute and I can't see anything but the blanket of trees around me and the mounds of snow on the brown grass and the silver-grey rocks and I can't hear anything but the whining of the wind in the trees; maybe nothing else exists. Maybe this green and windy place is the whole world.

I'm sweaty and cold at the same time. My breath is whistling inside my head. The wind blows through my jacket and my shoes are soaked from the snow. As we walk my cotton shirt starts to get clammy with moisture and I feel sticky and cold all over.

My shorts start to wrinkle all by themselves and the razor crease pressed into the front has disappeared. The shorts are loose but uncomfortable because they're starched cotton. Red. It seems as if every pair of shorts I ever owned were bright red. I wear them with white or pink T-shirts that have red somewhere in the pattern: usually wild swirls, butterflies, cats or fairies. What I really want is a pair of faded denim cutoffs so tight I wouldn't be able to bend over. My thin white legs protrude from the cuffed edges of my shorts and end in white and grey shoes that Mom washes with the bleach load in the laundry. They always smell of bleached rubber.

We're back in the trees and there is still no lake shining in the sun. The world is getting smaller, smaller. All it is now is the rhythm of walking: whuff, whuff, whuff, whuff and the small drum beat of my heart thump, thump, thumping. My feet are just moving, that's all. I don't think they would stop if I told them to. Whuff, whuff, whuff. Somewhere near but far away I vaguely hear voices talking in low tones. I think it is Mom and Dad.

Heavy, warm hands on my shoulders stop me moving. I look up at Dad and try to smile.

"You're tired, Pumpkin. Sit down." I look around.

Chloe and Matt are sprawled on an outcropping of rock. We haven't found the lake. There is snow all around us now. I brush the crusty snow from a fallen log and drop down near them. The sun is lower in the sky now and it flashes in and out of the heavy forest all around us.

Mom digs in the backpack for a bag of bright oranges. She gives us each one. They look so soothing and cheerful that I just hold mine for a while. Dad comes over and cuts a small slit in the skin for me with his jackknife. The sharp smell of the orange oil is so beautiful and bright in the blue air. My hands are bare and my legs are very cold now that we're not moving.

CHAPTER 9

WE CAN'T GET HOME FROM HERE

Quietly we sit and suck the sweet oranges and then lick the juice from our fingers. We watch silently as Dad carefully splits one of the plastic lunch bags along its seam, producing two squares of plastic. Mom takes these and comes over to me with a worried look on her face. I know that look. It scares me.

"What's the matter, Mom?", I ask softly as she kneels down beside me in the snow.

"Nothing, Honey," she says with a thin smile. "Give me your feet okay? We are going to play a game. We are going to pretend we are all Arctic explorers and we have to wear these special waterproof snow shoes to explore."

She takes one of my feet and strips off my trainer and my wet sock. She rubs my cold foot very hard with a pair of dry socks from the pack then puts them on and ties my shoe back on. Over this she wraps the plastic and secures it around my ankle with a strip torn from her scarf. Tired as I am I'm worried to see Mom tearing up her good scarf; it seems such a funny thing to be doing on a mountain. And then I notice my shoes! I grab my foot and turn it upside down to look at the bottom.

"What is that? Uagghhh! That's awful! What is it?" The white bottom of my shoe has turned a slimy pink-orange. So has the other one. So have Chloe's and Matt's.

"That's just snow mold. It's nothing to worry about."

"Yech! What's snow mold?"

"Fusarium nivale," says Matt. "We took it in school."

"I'm sure!" I grumble. "Tell me another one, smarty."

"It's just a growth," Mother says. "The snow never gets a chance to melt up this high and a special type of fungus grows on it. It won't hurt you."

"I knew that. You're so dumb, Joanie. What do you do in school all the time? Daydream?" snarls Chloe.

"I do not!" I howl, trying to hit her with my orange shoe. But I did feel stupid and I was so tired and cold I just wanted to go home.

"That's enough of that," Mom says. "We have something to talk about. Now be quiet. All of you."

"Your Mother and I have talked this over," Dad says, "And we have decided it would be best to try to go over the west shoulder of Castle Mountain to get back to the valley. The hiking book called this an afternoon hike but we may have slipped off the path somewhere near the ridge because there isn't any mention of this kind of terrain. We should have been at the lake an hour ago and we should be halfway back to the car by now."

I look at Mom and then at Matthew. Mom smiles reassuringly at me but Matt is just staring at the ground.

"Now don't worry. It just means that we miss seeing the lake and the back valley, that's all."

"Why don't we just turn around and go back the way we came?"

asks Chloe. We all turn to look behind us at the unbroken wall of trees.

"Dad," Matt asks very quietly. "Are we lost?"

My stomach drops down into my toes. Was that possible? Could Mom and Dad get lost? I remember being lost once on the bus when I went with Mom and Chloe to the dentist. I was daydreaming and didn't notice they had gotten off the bus. They didn't notice that I wasn't with them either. Suddenly I was all alone on the bus.

It was the most horrible feeling. I knew for sure that I would never, ever see Mom or Dad or Matt or Chloe ever again! I was all alone in the world! Then a lady on the bus who had seen what happened came over to me as I sat there crying. She took me by the hand and helped me off the bus at the next stop and she walked with me back the way the bus had come. Mom and Chloe were walking toward us the other way. Mom's face was so white I let go of the lady's hand and ran to her and threw my arms around her to let her know I was all right. I was even glad to see mean old Chloe. Mom cried and hugged me very tightly. Then she hugged the lady.

It was an adventure. I was kind of a hero for a while but I never forgot how it felt to be lost and alone.

And now maybe all of us are lost. But at least we aren't all alone; we have each other and I say so. Dad comes over and puts his hand on my shoulder and kisses the top of my head. For a tiny second I'm almost happy.

"Of course we aren't lost," he says. "You can't get lost in these mountains. You can always find the highway and the Bow River valley by getting to a high spot of land."

"Why don't we just turn around then?!" asked Chloe. "I'm tired and I'm cold." Mom is putting plastic snow shoes on Chloe and Matt. She has nothing left to tie Chloe's on with except elastic bands but she makes sure the bands are loose and tells Chloe to check them once in a while to make sure they're not cutting off her circulation.

I want to tease her about her feet turning blue and falling off but I don't because she looks so pale and scared.

"I'm tired and my feet hurt," grumbles Matt. I look at him in amazement. Macho Matt is complaining about being tired!?

"Let's quit this stupid hike and go back."

"Well now," says Dad, "You think about that for a minute. How long have we been walking? Over four hours, not counting the stop for lunch. It's 4:00 now. If we turn around, even though it will be downhill, it'll still take us another three hours to get back. It will be dark by then and I'm not sure you guys can make it that far anyway."

Chloe jumps up at that. "I can make it. It's just that lazy Joanie. She's the problem. Let's just leave her here."

"Chloe!" Dad says. "Joanie has been doing very well. In fact she has complained a whole lot less than you two have. That's not the point. The point is that your Mother and I feel it will be shorter and safer to try to cut across the shoulder and head directly for the highway. We must have left the path some time back and it might take us awhile to find it again. It'll be tougher walking this way but you guys are all fighters, right?"

"Right!" we grumble.

Mom gives us each a half a chocolate bar, even Chloe. She gives me a mean grin and bites deep into the chocolate. I'm too tired to even stick out my tongue at her.

Matt looks solemnly at his plastic covered feet with the red Safeway logo bright against the snow.

"You can walk with me, Joanie" he says and takes my hand.

CHAPTER 10

LOST

Silently we begin to trudge off through the snow and the solid woods. I look up at the Castle and it seems to be frowning down at me, with great ridges of black rock glowering above shining snow eyes.

I don't know how we can know where we're going. There is no hint of a path anymore; just grey snow and black trees and millions of tangled shadows. I am very cold.

It was warm when we left home this morning. The weather was supposed to be hot and sunny. We were all wearing light, summer clothes, never thinking we would actually be climbing in snow. I dream of warm woolen mittens and long, fleecy pants and my winter jacket with the imitation fur trim around the hood. I walk along beside Matt and a little behind him, letting him break the hard crust of the snow for me as we go.

The first bits of twilight are fluttering against the sky like something with wings waiting to drop suddenly on us and sweep us away into a world of blackness. Everything is absolutely still. Even the wind is holding its breath. The only light is a reflection of sunlight from the top of the Castle above us. Instead of hiking around the east shoulder to the lake behind the mountain, we seem to have climbed around the base of the shoulder and then got turned so that we climbed up the high shoulder onto the mountain itself. We can't tell much about where we are though. The whole world is filled with trees and snow.

I'm really tired. I keep falling asleep but my feet keep walking. It's a good thing they know what to do. Matt is not holding my hand anymore, he's far ahead, but I still follow the trail he cuts in the snow.

My legs are red and stinging, especially at a place above my socks where the hard edge of the snow keeps scraping. I step over and around bushes and lumps and, once or twice, I fall. I get up each time without complaining, I know there isn't any point;

there's nothing Mom and Dad can do to make this all go away. They are as lost as we are.

It makes me feel kind of strange to think that but, in a way, it makes me feel good too. I can't explain it. It's as if before Mom and Dad were perfect so you had to do what they told you without asking questions but all of a sudden it turns out they're people too, just like me. They get scared too. I could hear it in their voices even when they were telling us everything was all right.

I would like to hug them and tell them everything will be fine. I know it will. I know somehow that we are special and nothing truly horrible could happen to all my family at once. That wouldn't be fair. We'll get home. Somehow.

Suddenly I see a soft blue light among the trees! It flickers like a fire made of bluebells. There is a strange, sweet perfume in the air. I creep closer through the trees. There, in a small clearing, I see a hundred fairies dressed in swirling capes sitting, standing, moving around a blue, glowing fire. Some of them are cooking in tiny pots the size of thimbles, some are dancing to the music of a chorus of crickets dressed in tuxedos and playing on a tiny toadstool stage. It is obviously a very special occasion.

"Welcome" they cry when they see me, their tiny

voices sounding like the smallest of bells. "We've been waiting for you."

They make me sit down on a tree stump that's been hollowed out to form a throne. They cover me with a warm, velvet cloak. I smile.

"You have done well," I say. "The party is lovely and you have been successful today in rescuing the human family from a terrible death in the woods. And now one of you, who was especially brave today in fighting off the bears, will be knighted. Come forward, Sir Periwinkle."

Poof! The fairies are gone when there's a loud human shout ahead of me. I frown and squint into the gloom. Who dared scare my fairy world away? Ahead I see Matt standing on a ridge that looks like the end of everything; beyond him is only blue-black space sprinkled with a few early stars.

I forget my aching legs and my chattering teeth and scramble up to him. There is the valley we left so many long hours ago. It pours east and west of us into the horizon. Twilight is flapping full against the sky now like a huge, purple bird.

Far below us we can see the long golden eyes of cars on the highway. They seem very strange to me in my dizzy exhaustion. I can't seem to remember having seen anything like them in so very long.

"It's our car, Dad!" Matt cries. "There's the car." He is pointing down into the gloom. Far, far beneath our feet I can just make out a bare patch that might be a parking lot and a small, dark smear that could be a car.

"How do you know?" I try to ask him. Nothing comes out.

Dad comes up to us. He's panting shallowly like a dog and his face in the dusk is very pale and floats like a white balloon above my head.

"I think you're right, Pal," he says, putting his arm on Matt's shoulders. "By God, we're going to make it!"

I stare at him. I can't believe he ever doubted that we would. Mom and Chloe are crunching across the snow behind us. Chloe's face shines in the silver-blue light and it almost looks as though she has been crying. I say nothing.

And so we start down the mountain.

CHAPTER 11

DOWN, DOWN AND DOWN SOME MORE

And now it's straight down. We go over the ridge together like a reluctant army. Very carefully we start down the steep slope and immediately the view of the valley and the highway disappears in darkness again. The growth is so heavy that it's almost impossible to put one foot in front of the other. Fallen logs and underbrush cover every inch of ground. I fall back to stay away from the swishing slap of the branches as Matt and Dad struggle ahead pushing them aside.

There had been a little bit of light left at the top of the ridge but here among the heavy pine and spruce, struggling like rabbits through the evil undergrowth, we're working almost blind in the darkness.

At one point we come up to a fallen tree whose trunk is so enormous even Dad can't climb over it and it is too long to walk around. Finally Dad hoists Matt up to the top, then Chloe.

Between the two of them they are able to swing Mom up to the top then Dad lifts me and hands me to Mom on the top of the log. Those few seconds held tightly in his arms and listening to the comforting whump, whump of his heart against my ear...those warm seconds were enough to make my eyelids droop and I think I was asleep by the time Mom propped me on my feet on the other side of the log.

It scares me to think that Dad might be sick. He seems so thin and frail now and I don't remember him being that way. And he coughs a lot. Way more than normal. Nobody will tell me anything. They seem to think I can't guess. They seem to think if they don't talk about it then everything will be fine. I don't know what's wrong but something is and it scares me more, not knowing.

I try to think of something nice. I even try to think about school and my Geography test this week but I can't think of anything. I can't see anything. I don't think I can even feel anything except tired, tired, forever tired. My feet are so cold they have disappeared into the black ground. I no longer own them. I stumble and grab for branches and trees with bare hands that are skinned and raw. I don't even care if we run into a bear or a cougar or some other thing. If we do I'll just lie down and let it eat me. I don't care.

Black bristles whip across my face and the plastic is flapping in shreds around my wet shoes. Each step feels like an enormous job that I can't do but somehow I keep on doing. I can't hear the rest of my family around me in the woods anymore. They can't be far away. I reach out to grab Dad's hand though I know he isn't there.

Suddenly out of the endless shadows comes a shattering scream and at the same time the whole world tilts upside down and whirls past my eyes like the insides of a kaleidoscope gone crazy. I am spinning down through blankets of black knives. They cut at my face and legs and hair. Then an enormous trap opens up and snaps shut on my foot, twisting it under me in a sharp, agonizing jerk! With a sickening THUMP, the entire universe stopped whirling.

The pain in my leg is unbelievable. I lie there just feeling it; amazed at how much pain can exist in one place at one time. It seems like...not a dream really...

more like I have suddenly entered a black and terrible novel where terror lives in every blade of grass and every sinister shadow. My head shoots fire from one side to the other, above my eyes, in great blinding blasts of pain.

I take a deep breath and scream. It seems like the only natural thing I can do. I can't move but somehow I have to force some sort of activity out of the darkness and if all I can do is make noise then that's what I'll do. The screams sail up out of my mouth and away into the hard, black sky.

There are three silver stars winking above the tallest tree. They're laughing. So calm and peaceful. They can't hear me. No one can hear me. I am utterly alone. I have never, ever been so alone.

I think of my family sitting safely at home watching The Crown, drinking hot chocolate. I can hear them say, "I wonder where Joanie is tonight? I wonder if she will ever come home."

And I want to. I really want to. They're my family and they love me. Without them I am just a lost girl on a mountain. Without them I'll lie here alone the whole night. I'll see the sun come up once more and I'll lie here and watch it paint the soft colors of morning on the sky above my head and then I will die. And they'll never know.

I notice I'm not screaming anymore. I'm afraid that any sound will bring a wolf with bright eyes and long teeth. I hear a crashing sound in the woods. I lie still, staring into the darkness. My ankle throbs with hot pain. I don't dare even breathe! It's coming for me!

CHAPTER 12

CUT LOOSE

A voice. Human. Not a bear or wolf.

"Joanie?!?! Where are you?" It's Chloe crashing through a blackberry bush behind my head. She struggles with the bush so hard that the brambles are cutting her and I can see her hands and face have streaks of shiny black blood.

"Chloe I'm here," I cry.

"Joanie! Joanie! Joanie!" Her tears are wet on my face and, in spite of the pain, I stare up at her white face in the muffled darkness. This isn't my big sister. There is no way she would ever care if I got hurt. I can't believe she is crying.

"She's here!" Chloe yells in a thick voice. "Dad, Mom. Help!"

I can hear more crashing above us and Mom's voice yelling through the darkness, "Don't move her! Joanie, don't move!"

Matt comes tumbling out of the blackness and Chloe puts an arm out to stop him tripping over me. Then Dad is there beside us.

"Joan, can you move your leg at all?" he asks, and I suddenly realize I haven't even tried. I try to move my foot just a little but my leg is caught in the teeth of some huge animal and it won't let go. Pain flares all the way up from my foot to my hip.

"What about your arms?"

They work when I try them but my leg…I start to gulp for air.

"Okay, don't panic, Honey," Dad says. "Chloe, reach in my backpack and get out my knife. That's good."

"Now, can you slide under your sister here and hold her head and shoulders off the cold ground? I'm going to try to cut some of this stuff around her leg."

I lift my head a bit and Chloe slides in under my head and shoulders. Her lap is warm and soft. She strokes my hair with a cold hand and is mumbling something over and over.

Dad cuts at the things that are wound around my foot. It hurts so much I grab Chloe's hand and squeeze it tight to keep from yelling. She would laugh if I yelled like a baby. I am crying though. I can't help it. I can feel the cold tears pouring down my cheeks and into the neck of my light jacket.

Then Mom is there. "Take it easy," she says to Dad. "Don't move her foot, it looks broken. No, don't straighten it. When you get it free I'll wrap it to stabilize it but if we try to straighten it we might do more damage."

Her voice is almost unrecognizable to me. It is so high and squeaky with tension. In the dull grey light from a bit of moon rising beyond the trees I watch her strip off the only jacket she is wearing. Now she is shivering in a light cotton shirt.

"Mom, don't."

"It's okay, sweetie. We have to get you out of this."

Dad finally has me free and Chloe helps pull me out of the tangle of juniper bushes while Mom holds my foot to keep it still. She very gently wraps the warm fleece jacket around my ankle and ties it on with the arms. The tiny bit of warmth is amazing. I take a deep breath. The air is thick with the smell of bruised juniper.

Dad takes off his backpack and hands it to Matt. Then my big brother helps our mother lift me onto

Dad's back and I cling tightly to his thin shoulders.

"John! You can't. Not in your condition," Mom gasps.

"No choice, Honey," he grunts as he settles my legs around his waist. "She sure as heck can't walk."

Mom is quiet as she ties my leg around his waist with his belt so that my foot won't bang against him when he walks.

"All set there, soldier?" Dad asks.

"All set," I say through gritted teeth.

CHAPTER 13

WE SOLDIER ON

And then we start off again. This time we must look like a little army in retreat with our wounded being transported to the nearest hospital unit. Bravely the wounded soldier clenches her jaw and fights back the pain. She will not endanger her friends by showing the slightest sign of weakness. No, she would be brave and silent to the end.

I can hear Matt moving ahead, "This way, Dad. Watch that hole. There's a slippery patch here." He is the guiding light. I will recommend him for a medal when we get back.

Chloe trudges silently right beside me with a hand on my back, ready to steady me if I slip. I'm glad the bears didn't get her after all. She's part of the family and if any one of us wasn't here anymore, the rest of us would have an awful empty space in our lives where that person had been. The next time she hits me or steals my silver locket I'm going to try to remember that she is still family and that I really don't want her to die or anything.

"Almost there, Troops," gasps Dad. "Almost there. I can smell the coffee from here."

He coughs fitfully. I feel the little explosions in his chest. Dad is stumbling a lot more now and I want to tell him to put me down. I'm sure I can walk if I just lean on Chloe and limp a lot. I can't say anything though. Everything is swimming in front of me and I have to concentrate very hard not to get sick over Dad's shoulder.

I can hear him wheezing. The air going in and out of his chest sounds like a cat scratching its claws on a couch. What would we do if we had to be a family without Dad? I close my eyes tightly and try not to think about it.

Suddenly Matt shouts something. I can't hear what he's saying. Chloe pats my back gently.

"We're down," she says. "Matt's made it to the parking lot. You're going to be all right."

Guided by Matt's voice, we keep moving through the silver gloom of the forest until, finally, we break from the trees into a pool of moonlight. Over Dad's shoulder I can see the shining bulk of our car sitting alone in the parking lot. It looks beautiful.

I'm happy and so relieved but somehow, now that I know we really aren't going to die, I realize how terribly cold and hungry I am. And my leg hurts so much. Annoying little moans are coming out of my mouth.

Matt and Chloe must feel like that too because as soon as we get to the car Matt starts whining.

"Don't we have anything to eat in the car? How come you never bring any snacks for when we get back, Ma?"

As Dad lays me gently in the back seat of the car, Chloe starts to whine too.

"What a baby! Why does she always get the special treatment? If it was me had hurt my foot, I'd still have to take care of myself. I would have had to walk!"

"I would if I could," I snap. "But it hurts a lot and I can't even stand on it so I sure can't walk."

At this point Mom begins to laugh. At least I think it's a laugh but it sounds kind of hysterical. More like the wild screeching of monkeys in the zoo. We all stare at her. She laughs and laughs at us. Finally Dad gets up from where he is resting in the front seat. He walks over to her and, when he puts his arms around her, her laughing turns into crying. We are totally stunned. I look at Chloe to see what she thinks about this. Mom is actually crying real tears and I have never seen her do that before. I don't think my brother or sister have either. Matt's staring at his shoes with that really embarrassed look he gets when any of us get emotional. Chloe stands there, looking all dirty and messy, and staring at Mom with her mouth hanging open and her eyes wide and worried. Matt clears his throat really loud. He goes around the other side of the car and gets in near my head. I can't help noticing he's managed to sit by the window again even though there's nothing to see at this time of night.

Mom wipes her eyes after a minute and blows her nose. She whispers to Dad, "I'm okay now, John." Then in her normal controlled voice she says, "Well, we are down anyway."

She takes a deep breath and says, "You kids better take off those wet shoes and dry your feet off. You can use the emergency blanket then we'll cover our patient with it when you're done. I'll deal with your shoes, Joanie."

She stops talking then and looks at us for a minute.

Chloe and Matt struggle over the blanket. I lie there shivering uncontrollably.

"You know," she sighs as she tucks the emergency blanket snuggly around me. "I was really proud of you kids for a while back there. You were really good once the hard part began but now listen to you, whining and bickering like magpies."

"She's right, Troops," Dad says. "That was probably the worst mess we've ever been in, but I never heard one whimper from my three soldiers until now. I'm proud of you, too. All of you." His face looks grey in the moonlight. I'm not sure if it is just the shadows of the night.

"Matt," says Mom. "Your Father is in no condition to drive and I think I should be back here with our patient. You'll have to drive. We head for the hospital first before we go home."

CHAPTER 14

MATT GETS PROMOTED

Matt gets back out of the car and walks to the driver's side. He squares his shoulders in such a comical way I think I want to laugh but it comes out as a moan instead. At that Chloe scurries into the back seat and lays my head gently on her lap. Mom gets in the other side, carefully holding my injured foot.

Matt manages to start the car on the second try and we are moving.

"Well," Dad turns to look back at us. "We sure had an adventure today, didn't we?"

Nobody answers.

It feels very strange to me to be moving without my legs doing the walking when that's all they've done all day. I lie in the dark and feel Chloe's breathing against the side of my head. My head feels huge and I look down and my feet seem to be miles away. The inside of the car is not big enough to hold my huge body. I recognize this feeling, sometimes it happens at night when I'm really tired but can't sleep. If I let it go on too long I can make myself throw up from being so dizzy. I don't think that's a good idea right now so I shake my head to get the feeling to go away. Mom thinks I am in pain.

"I have some aspirins with me, Honey, if it hurts a lot," she says.

"It's okay," I groan. After all, I'm a soldier aren't I? I've been wounded in battle but I'm strong. I've been wounded before; this is nothing. It'll mean another purple heart. I laugh bravely through the pain, looking down at all the other medals on my chest as they gleam in the moonlight. I AM strong. I don't have to prove it to anyone. I take all the medals off, one by one, and throw them out the window where they flash through the night and drop, silently, into the glassy shine of the Elbow river that flows along beside the highway at this point.

My favorite teacher told us once that if you pretend to feel a certain way or be a certain way, eventually you do feel that way and you become that person. Your job is to figure out what kind of person you want yourself to be.

I watch the black wall of Castle Mountain slowly pass and swallow the moon. The trees on either side of the highway march in tight, black rows along the edge of the sky. I snuggle down into the warmth of the blanket and try to pretend it's not my ankle that's throbbing like that. I'm dizzy with the pain and my mind wanders like an abandoned dog.

My thoughts wander back to the horrible question I asked myself earlier. What if we didn't have Dad. What if something is seriously wrong and something happens to him? Can we make it without him? Mom is strong. And smart. We all see that strength every day. Matt just got a promotion to being able to drive. Chloe and I can help out more around the house. I know I should anyway.

I pretend I'm a deer lying in the forest, shot by a hunter, waiting to die. My poor little deer friends and family stand in the trees with just their huge soft eyes shining their sorrow; unable to do anything to help me but not wanting to leave me alone to face death. 'Thank you all for staying by my side,' I whisper.

The sadness of the scene makes the tears start

rolling down my face again. They soak into Chloe's blue jean shorts right under my cheek. She has her head lying back against the back of the seat and I think she's asleep. I'm glad because maybe she won't notice.

But I'm wrong. I feel a squeeze and notice, for the first time, that I'm holding my sister's hand. It gives me kind of a warm feeling when she squeezes my hand like that. We'll probably be arguing again tomorrow about just anything at all but for now she's my big sister.

I can see the back of Matt's head, bent tensely over the wheel. Mom's face, calm and controlled, is turned to the window but her hands are cradling my ankle in her lap. I hear Dad's low voice from the front seat guiding Matt as he makes a turn a little too sharply.

Mom turns to look at us in the dark car. "Your father's right, it was an adventure. It went a little sideways, I'll admit, but we made it. And things like this make you stronger and better able to deal with other situations that go wrong for you."

"I'm just glad we made it at all," Chloe mumbles.

I am too. And I know if we got through this together then we can get through anything.

Other Books By This Author

Women Without Shadows

A collection of poetry exploring women's lives and their journey from living under the shadow of someone else to emerging from the shadows and into the light of their own strength. A slim volume of gentle and powerful poems, each poem telling a small story of its own.

Journey To Night Mountain

A delightful tale of self-discovery; a fantasy story in the tradition of Alice in Wonderland; a frolic through cultural references that will resonate with anyone who remembers the golden era of the 50's, 60's and 70's; and a touching story of friendship all wrapped up in the strange world of a future that we can only wish could come true.

The One-Eyed Chevrolet
[Stories From Cougar Lake]

Nestled in the rolling foothills, where the prairie climbs to meet the Rocky Mountains, lies the small town of Cougar Lake. In this book all the doors in town swing quietly open for the reader to peer inside. Each inhabitant's life and story intersects with others like overlapping ripples in the water. Each story stands alone but each story reaches tendrils into others. The residents form a cast of beguiling, sometimes eccentric, characters each with their unique lives, loves and longings, their histories and their dreams. We learn what brought them to Cougar Lake and, more importantly, what keeps them here. In the end the town stands together to survive.

Books can be ordered from the author at: KathrynHartley.com

About The Author

Kathryn has had a life-long love affair with creative writing since she won her first poetry competition at age 10. She has published short stories and poetry in literary journals and anthologies over the years. Her work, both short fiction and poetry, has also been featured frequently on CBC Radio's Alberta Anthology program.

Professionally she served as the Executive Director of the Calgary Region Arts Foundation for 23 years. Then she and her husband and son moved from Calgary to Nelson in search of a more natural life style surrounded by lakes to paddle, trails to walk, and mountains and valleys to explore.

In Nelson Kathy worked for the Nelson and District Arts Council for two years then retired to concentrate on writing and many volunteer positions. She lives with her husband and two Chihuahuas in the serene lakeside town nestled in the gentle green mountains of southern British Columbia.

Contact:
Email: cougarlake2021@gmail.com
Website: www.KathrynHartley.com